MY FIRST LITTLE
MOTHER GOOSE

Illustr...
Lucinda M...

 A GOLDEN BOOK • NEW YORK

Golden Books Publishing Company, Inc., New York, New York 10106

Pat-a-cake, pat-a-cake, baker's man,
Bake me a cake as fast as you can.
Roll it and pat it and mark it with a *B*,
And put it in the oven for Baby and me.

Ring around the rosey,
A pocket full of posies.
Ashes! Ashes!
We all fall down!

Mary, Mary, quite contrary,
How does your garden grow?
With silver bells and cockleshells,
And pretty maids all in a row!

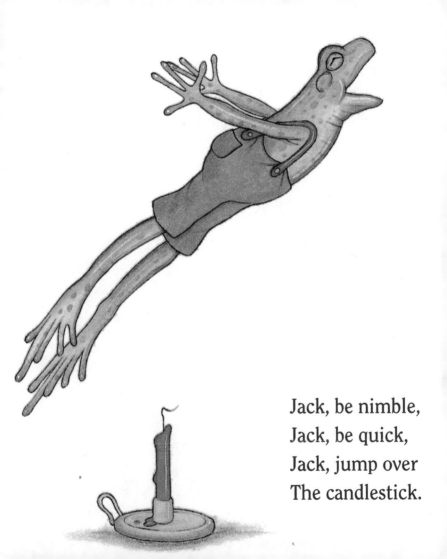

Jack, be nimble,
Jack, be quick,
Jack, jump over
The candlestick.

Polly, put the kettle on.
Polly, put the kettle on.
Polly, put the kettle on.
We'll all have tea.

It's raining, it's pouring,
The old man is snoring.
He went to bed and bumped his head,
And he didn't get up 'til morning.

Little Boy Blue,
Come blow your horn!
The sheep's in the meadow,
The cow's in the corn.

But where is the boy
Who looks after the sheep?
He's under the haystack,
Fast asleep.

Hickory, dickory, dock,
The mouse ran up the clock.
The clock struck one,
The mouse ran down.
Hickory, dickory, dock.

Humpty Dumpty sat on a wall,
Humpty Dumpty had a great fall.
All the king's horses
And all the king's men
Couldn't put Humpty Dumpty together again.

Once I saw a little bird
Come hop, hop, hop.
And I said, "Little bird,
Won't you stop, stop, stop?"

I was going to the window
To say, "How do you do?"
But she shook her little tail,
And away she flew.

This little piggy went to market,

This little piggy stayed home.

This little piggy had roast beef,

This little piggy had none.

And this little piggy cried,
"Wee, wee, wee, wee!"
All the way home.

Oh, do you know the muffin man,
The muffin man, the muffin man?
Oh, do you know the muffin man
Who lives in Drury Lane?

Jack Sprat could eat no fat,
His wife could eat no lean.
And so betwixt them both, you see,
They licked the platter clean.

Pease porridge hot,
Pease porridge cold,
Pease porridge in the pot,
Nine days old.

Some like it hot,
Some like it cold,
Some like it in the pot,
Nine days old.

There was an old woman
Lived under the hill,
And if she's not left,
She lives there still.

MRS
MOLE

Hickety, pickety, my black hen,
She lays eggs for gentlemen.
Sometimes nine, sometimes ten,
Hickety, pickety, my black hen.

"Pussy cat, pussy cat,
Where have you been?"
"I've been to London
To visit the queen."

"Pussy cat, pussy cat,
What did you there?"
"I frightened a little mouse
Under the chair."

Old Mother Hubbard
Went to the cupboard
To fetch her poor dog a bone.

But when she got there,
The cupboard was bare,
And so the poor dog had none.

Rain, rain, go away,
Come again another day.
Little Susie wants to play.
Rain, rain, go away.

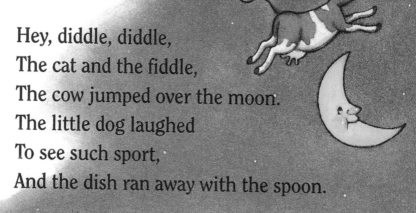

Hey, diddle, diddle,
The cat and the fiddle,
The cow jumped over the moon.
The little dog laughed
To see such sport,
And the dish ran away with the spoon.

Little Bo-Peep has lost her sheep,
And doesn't know where to find them.
Leave them alone, and they'll come home,
Wagging their tails behind them.

Twinkle, twinkle, little star,
How I wonder what you are!
Up above the world so high,
Like a diamond in the sky.
Twinkle, twinkle, little star,
How I wonder what you are!